ADVENTURES OF JOEY, ANDY AND LITTLE BIRD

A Pirate's Treasure

Written and Illustrated by
CAPT. JOHNATHAN HILLSTRAND

Peanut Butter Publishing

Seattle, Washington
Portland, Oregon
Denver, Colorado
Vancouver, B.C.
Scottsdale, Arizona
Minneapolis, Minnesota

ISBN: 978-1-59849-149-4

Library of Congress Control Number: 2013906938

Printed in the United States of America

Design: Soundview Design Studio

For individual, institutional or educational orders contact:
www.timebandit.tv

Requests for such permissions should be addressed to:

Peanut Butter Publishing
943 NE Boat Street
Seattle, Washington 98105
206-860-4900
www.peanutbutterpublishing.com

This book is dedicated to my loving family and friends. Thomas Oliver Doty (December 10th 1992 – December 19th, 2012.) And two great loving fathers, John W. Hillstrand and Robert Phillips.

One morning Joey and Andy Crabs went with their mother to pick up their father from work for the first time.

When they got there, they were very surprised. Their father was the great pirate Daddy Long Legs, and his first mate was the legendary Little Bird.

Pappa Crabs knew how much both boys wanted to be pirates. So when he told them he was staying home with Mother Crabs, and they could be Little Bird's first mates, they couldn't believe their little crab ears!

Just like that, the boys were both pirates, and Little Bird was the captain of his own ship, the *Daddy Crabs*.

He gave the three boys a treasure map and said, "If you follow the dotted line it will lead you to the greatest treasure in the world."

"Wow!" exclaimed Andy.

"What?" said Joey.

And all Little Bird could say was, "Squawk!"

As they sailed out of Safe Harbor, they opened the map. All they had to do was follow the dotted lines to the treasure! "Well, how hard could that be?" Joey asked.

Bridge over Troubled Waters

Troubled Waters

Octopus Garden

Crybaby eyes Cape

Ship Wreck PIRATE OCEAN

Ship Wreck

SAFE HARBOR

MORE
Troubled
WATERS
HOT
WATERS
Snotty
Nose
Point
Monster
BAY
Stinky
Smelly
cove
SHIP
WRECK
N
W
E
S
Pirate
ISLAND
Treasure
Island

The next day the three little pirates decided to look for Junior, a legendary navigator. He would surely help them find the treasure. They asked two penguins how to get to Junior's house at Octopus Gardens under the sea.

The penguins told them to go past Crybaby Eyes Cape, and Octopus Gardens would be just before the Bridge Over Troubled Waters.

"Well hey! How hard could that be?" asked Joey.

As they sailed to Junior's, a huge storm rolled in. The waves started getting bigger and crashing over the sides of the ship.

Joey and Andy were a little scared, but Little

Bird said, "Don't worry! I'll get us through this!"
"Hang on!" he yelled as another wave hit their
ship. It was going to be a long night!

The next morning the storm was gone and they had made it to Junior's.

They watched
some sea lions and
polar bears fishing
while Junior got ready.

With Junior on board, the four young pirates were on their way to find the world's greatest treasure! All they had to do was go through Troubled Waters, then More Troubled Waters, past Snotty Nose Point and Monster Bay, around Stinky Smelly Cove, and then they would be in sight of Treasure Island.

"Well alrighty! How hard could that be?" Joey asked again.

Suddenly a huge sea monster came out of nowhere and bumped the ship! "No, no, please stop!" yelled Little Bird.

The sea monster replied, "I'm only trying to scratch my back. I won't hurt you! There used to be

a lot of ships that sailed through here, but I guess there's a sea monster around attacking ships, so I never see anyone anymore!"

"OK, you can scratch your back!" they said.

No one had the heart to tell him that he was probably the sea monster. What a nice fellow they all thought, as they sailed away.

ext they saw two tufted puffins boxing on an ice flow. They were practicing for the Puffin Olympics. Little Bird told them about their adventure so far, and where they were going. The puffins wished them luck and started boxing again.

Little Bird said, "Well boys, we're only about a day away from Treasure Island!"

"Only a day away! Ha! How hard could that be?" Joey Crabs replied.

The next day, out of nowhere, a school of attacking bully fish appeared. They were prehistoric looking with very big, sharp teeth. They were jumping and snapping at everyone on the ship!

Little Bird yelled, "Man your stations!
Grab the slingshots!"

Andy and Joey sprang into action, shooting sponge balls at the fish. Next to them stood Junior with four slingshots, and Little Bird with his sponge cannon. Fish and sponge balls were flying everywhere!

All four pirates stood their ground. Then, suddenly, the bully fish were gone. If Daddy Long Legs could have seen them, he would have been very proud.

They all cheered, "That was close!" They did a little pirate jig as they threw their hats in the air. Then they saw it . . . Treasure Island. It was off their bow!

"We made it!" Joey cheered. "Now all we have to do is dig up the treasure! How hard could that be?"

They all looked at each other and started laughing. Wow, what an adventure, but it wouldn't be over until they got their hands on that treasure!

They couldn't believe it. There it was . . .
the treasure! Just like the map showed,
it was on the X,
under the big W.

What wonderful treasure could it be? Gold or silver?
Maybe it was full of candy! They all jumped off the
ship to dig it up!

They dug the treasure chest up. They opened the lock. "What?" they yelled, "Baby pictures?"

"It's full of old baby pictures!"

"We came all the way for this?"

"That's Pappa's treasure?"

"Yes," Andy said, "Can't you see, Joey? It's full of pictures of you and me. WE are Pappa's treasure! It's not gold. It's not silver — or even candy. It's memories, and the love of family and friends!"

That's the world's greatest treasure . . . it's US, Love, Family, and Friends!

The End!

To get a copy of this book, as well as the other adventures of Little Bird and Joey and Andy Crabs, go to **timebandit.tv**